SOMETHING WORTHWHILE

By

Lucius Agee

To the descendants

of Lucius and Aline Agee

Rob

Robert, at age 12, seemed to find trouble everywhere, at home, at school and the neighborhood. His parents were usually aggravated by his behavior and were constantly after him to be different, to stop doing this or that and start doing other things. Everybody called him Rob and he usually answered but sometimes he just ignored the call.

When a new neighbor moved into the vacant rental house down the street Rob's curiosity urged him to ride his bike by several times to see who was there and what might be happening. At first, he could see no one but on his fifth ride-by he heard a sound coming from the garage, so he turned his bike into the gravel drive. He knew the sound he heard was a machine, but it was not one he could identify. He peeked in between the doors that weren't latched and was spotted by the man looking straight back at him.

"Come on in," he called. "My name's Delbert. What's yours?"

"Ron. What cha doin'?"

"I'm making my old Shepherd a new doghouse. I just left the old one when we moved and thought he deserved a new house too. Look at this and see what you think."

Delbert showed him a drawing of a doghouse with the dimensions labeled on each part. Then he showed him a plank he was getting ready to saw and showed him how to use a square and a flat pencil to mark a straight line across the plank after he measured. Ron had studied measurements in arithmetic at school but this was the first time he had seen any sense in learning about inches and fractions. Sure, he had fooled around with a ruler measuring things just for fun, but this measuring seemed important. Ron watched Delbert saw straight across the mark and held the boards steady for Delbert to nail together.

Seeing that Ron was careful and interested, Delbert asked, "Do you want to hammer in the nail in the next one?"

Ron held the nail carefully and hoped he wouldn't hit his finger. At first he hit the nail lightly but Delbert urged him to hit harder. He pounded it in while Delbert held the planks steady. Seeing the boy so happy with the work, Delbert complimented him. "Boy, you're gonna be good at building things. Do you want to make something to take home?"

"Yeah, but what can I build? I don't have any wood.

Delbert showed him a stack of boards and explained, "These are my scraps from other things I made. I think we can find enough for a bird house. Do you want to make a bird house?"

"I sure do, but I don't know how make anything." answered Ron.

"Don't worry about that. I'm gonna help you! First, we have to make a plan and draw it out. Look over there and pull out a few planks about a foot long and let's see what we have to work with," Delbert said with a pat on the boy's shoulder.

They looked through the scraps of wood and selected a short stack of planks that were long enough for the sides of a bird house. Next Delbert picked up a tablet and pencil and sat in the only chair in the garage and motioned for Ron to sit on the stack of planks near enough to watch. He made a simple sketch and asked Ron, "How does this suit you??

Ron grinned and said it was fine.

Delbert penciled in the dimensions of each side piece, the bottom and the top. He explained that he needed two boards cut to be the exact size for the sides and two more identical in size for the front and back. More boards for the roof and floor were cut and set aside. Ron wondered how the birds would get in and out of the house but soon found out when Delbert took a special saw and cut hole in one of the boards for the birds to enter and exit.

Ron was alarmed when he heard his name called to come home for supper but Delbert explained, "We'll finish it after school tomorrow, Go on home and don't' get in trouble and we'll finish it and paint it."

"Do you promise?"

"Yeah, now git on home and I'll see you tomorrow. Now what color do you think the birds in your yard would like?" Delbert gave him a little shoulder squeeze and eased him out through the door.

" Yellow! Bye!" yelled Ron as he jumped on his bike and started for home, thinking he would look in the

encyclopedia to see if birds liked one color better than another. He wanted his birds to be happy.

The next day after school, Ron changed to his play clothes in record time and started out the door. His mom grabbed his arm and said, "Wait! Where are you going in such a hurry?"

"Just down the street." Ron answered.

"Not until you take the trash out, young man! And you didn't get anything to eat. Are you hungry?"

Ron grabbed the trash sack from under the sink with one hand and a handful of crackers with other, not bothering to add the peanut butter his mama had placed on the table for him. "See you after while, Mama," Ron yelled as he rushed down off the back porch to the drop the trash bag into the can, jumped on his bike and sped down the street.

Delbert grinned when Ron entered the garage and got right to work putting the birdhouse together and boring a hole to insert a little round stick for the perch just below the entrance hole. The yellow paint was waiting, so , after watching Delbert dip the brush into the paint and stroke it on one side, Ron took the brush and finished it. They decided to change the color to green for the roof that extended a little farther in the front.

That project was the first of many that filled the after-school hours for several days and on Saturdays. He took his teacher a bird house for a present and she and the other kids were impressed that he had make it himself. He felt especially self-confident and happy when his mama almost cried about the small wall shelf he brought home as a present for her.

The day Ron's dad appeared at the door of the garage workshop, Delbert stood and waited for an angry voice, but it didn't come. Instead, Ron's dad said, "Delbert, I'm Jake,

Ron's daddy. I took off work early today so I can talk to you when Ron isn't here. I don't know how you did it, by my boy is a changed boy, And for the good! He's a happier kid and really enjoys coming down here with you. He used to gripe and complain and be stubborn about doing his chores but now he does them in a hurry to get to come in here with you. I really thank you."

"You have a good boy there," responded Delbert. "If I had a boy like that, I would try to do some things with him."

"I actually can't do anything like you're doing. Would you let me come every now and then and let me learn a little bit, too? I work in an office and I don't even know what some of the things you have in here do."

"Well, I think that would be fine, Jake, but only if you take both of us fishing one afternoon," Delbert replied with a grin, thinking he might do a little changing, too.

As they shook hands, Ron walked in the door with a grin that showed he had heard the last part of the conversation.

Cutting Firewood

The morning was warm but with just enough nip in the air to remind Mama that the leaves would soon turn to bright colors. Ned and Ben headed for the woods with their dog, Homer, carrying a crosscut saw and an ax on their shoulders. Their plan was to find a tree to cut for stove wood. When their dad was alive, he had always cut enough wood to keep the house warm and the kitchen stove sup plied. The boys had watched the process and learned to use a saw and ax but this was the first time to go without him. But now it was up to them to help Mama.

"Boys, we need to start thinking about how to get wood for the cookstove and for the fireplace. We sure don't want to wait until it snows to get it. Your daddy always cut in the summer and stacked it to dry out some before we needed it.

"It ain't raining today, Mama, so it won't have to dry out." said seven year old Ben.

"Silly, she means the sap inside the tree is wet, not the outside. I won't burn so good when it's green and the sap is still runing."

Ned felt like a grown-up instead of the twelve-year-old he was at the moment, but the feeling was a temporary. He knew they had a man's job to do and a strong will.

He continued talking to his mama, "Me and Ben will go get the wood today."

"I'll go with you." Mama declared.

"Nope, this is man's work. You hav'ta can all those beans canned today that you picked yesterd'y. Daddy showed us how, so we can do it without you." Being boys, aged ten and seven, Ned and Ben were eager to get out by themselves to use their dad's tools.

Mama knew their dad had showed them a thing or two about saws and axes and always had shown them the safe way to handle tools that could do great damage to a finger or leg. She couldn't help by remind them, "Boys, remember what your daddy said about being careful. You can get hurt really bad if you don't watch what you are doing."

As much as she hated to watch her two sons go off by themselves, she calmed herself down and got busy snapping green beans into shorter pieces to fit into the jars she had already washed for canning.

Homer darted away from them sniffing to the edge of the woods for scents of wildlife, then back he would rush to check on his boys who pulled an old rusted red wagon. The wagon had holes but would still hold a good amount of wood it they stacked it right. A path with weeds choking in made pulling the wagon possible but took some muscle. Granddaddy, who lived just down the lane, had a mule and wagon that could haul a huge load but the brothers had decided to do this on their own.

"Hey, Ben look up there. That's a good 'un." exclaimed Ned as he pointed to a nice tree on a ledge of a small bluff about halfway up. The bluff was about twelve feet up from the ground where they stood.

"But how're we gonna get up there?" questioned Ben.

"The same way that wild cat I heard last night got up there. We'll climb up over there where the slope is and walk the ledge." Ned said with a straight face and listened for a reaction.

"I ain't goin' up where no wild cat was! I'm goin' home!" yelled Ben and he started running back the same path. Ned chased him down yelling as he ran, "Wait, wait, wait! I was just teasing. There ain't no wildcats around here. I need you to help me. Come on. Let's get that tree. Mama needs it."

After leaving the wagon, they climbed up the slope on all fours, partly carrying and partly dragging the saw and ax, and reached the ledge to discover was about ten feet wide, more room than they had expected. The tree was Lynnwood, an exceptionally light soft wood, and not much good for a fireplace because it burns too hot and fast, but it was perfect for their mother's kitchen cookstove. They knew their mother would be tickled to have a quick burning wood to heat her oven and make her pot of beans boil.

They cut the tree and made it fall toward the side of the bluff and easily trimmed off the green limbs with the sharp ax and watched the sap drip from the cut. The two boys worked as a team to pull the crosscut teeth across the trunk of the tree to section it off into ten-foot-long logs. They decided to get the logs off the ledge before using the ax to split the logs into firewood sticks.

They had no experience getting logs down off a cliff and thought they would just throw them down, but the logs were heavy, being full of sap, and there was a risk of them rolling to who knows where. They stood and searched the ledge for the best place to throw off the logs and decided the slope they had climbed up was the logical place to roll them down because a big oak stood at the bottom. If they were lucky the logs would land against the oak tree trunk and not scatter all over the place. The slope was about twenty feet to the side of where they stood. To get logs that far would be heavy work and risky without much spare room to wiggle the logs to the slope.

Standing up and looking over the edge, Ned dreaded the attempt, and watched Ben kick sticks off the ledge. Noticing the bark on one long white log was beginning to peel off, Ned gave it a tug and it released from the trunk easily. Then the idea hit.

Ned explained, "Look, Ben! This bark is tough but it comes off easy."

They pulled the bark off half the trunk, the entire ten-foot length in one long piece, and laughed at the wet sap all along the length of it. A slide would be much easier than lifting and throwing.

Moving the long piece of bark carefully into place toward the slope, they rolled one log onto the wet sap and gave it a push. The runway worked! The logs slipped easily along with nudges from the boys. When it got to the slope, down it fell and rolled all the way to the bottom of the bluff. The next log soon followed. They laughed each time a long log fell and lodged against the oak tree, knowing their idea had saved them from heavy lifting and carrying. As their daddy use to say, "That's using your noggin'!"

At the bottom of the bluff, the work continued until they had cut the logs into short pieces with the saw and split them into pieces that would fit into their mother's cookstove. They were glad the straight logs split easily and straight. They loaded some of the stove wood on to their wagon and took it home but left some to get later. They felt too tired and starving to do it all in one day.

The stove wood was placed in the hot sun for the sap to dry before it was ready to burn. Their mama was proud of her two sons who supplied her with stove wood that lit quickly and burned hot, just right for her to brown the biscuits to fill their bellies. She laughed as they told her of the slippery slide they invented to make the work lighter and quicker. Now they had time to play a little football before dark set in. They were never too tired for a little play,

Just Boys Playing

Gone Swimming

The brothers, J. P. and Jim loved swimming in the creek
and often headed to their favorite swimming hole. It was called
Rocky Hole because of a big rock in the deepest part. They had
to be careful and not hit the rock and knock their brains out
when they dived off the bank.

On the bank of the creek were some tall horse weeds
about nine feet tall. They were about six inches apart, so thick
they could not walk through them without taking some down .
The sun was hot and they had shed their clothes and left them at
the edge of the weeds. They needed some shade. They cut the
horse weeds out at the ground about six foot out at the ground
about six-foot square and hung the cut weeds across the
standing weeds to form a roof. They sat back in the shade of the
weeds when they go out of the creek for a rest from swimming.

One day when they were in the creek with only their
heads above the water, they heard some girls talking. The creek
ran over some big flat rocks before the deep hole. They knew

the girls would come to the flat rocks, but they didn't have time to get out and escape. The girls were on a field trip with their Sunday school teacher but the girls knew where they wanted to go, right to the flat rocks to wade but when they saw the boys they kept standing there talking to the boys under water with the heads out. The boys couldn't get out because they did not have on a stitch. The teacher , knowing the boys' predicament finally insisted the girls leave. The only clothes the boys had were overalls, no shirt or shoes, but they were glad to have them back on for the walk home.

Watching the Train

Instead of going home, J.P and Jim decided to go watch the train and see who got on and off. It was a steam engine and made a lot of noise. It was the most exciting thing around and they watched it almost every day. The big engine huffing and puffing out smoke and steam was a powerful thing to see pulling all those cars on two little rails. Those rails gave the boys a place to walk between the hills when the train had gone by and another wouldn't come for hours.

Sling Shots

After the train ran, the boys decided to go work on their sling shot. J P.'s friend had given them an on old red inner tube that was no longer suitable for a tire. It was made of real rubber and would stretch just right for a sling shot. They went to their grandfather's farm and into the woods looking for a forked branch with a good shape and size. After getting the right forks they used their pocketknives to clean it up and notch near the ends of the Y for the rubber bands. The rubber bands were very important. It had to be real rubber and the length to match the user. The width of the band determined its strength. The width also had be just the right strength for the user.

J. P. and Jim fit the rubber bands to the forked sticks and stuck them in their back pockets. They pulled them out and shot at a lot of things. Over the next few days they became good shots. As they went down the railroad tracks, the insulators on the telephone poles made a good target. After hitting several and breaking several they felt guilty and quit.

One day at the creek, J. P. saw a blue heron glide behind a big rock. The heron would stick his head up and dip it back down. J.P. drew back his sling shot band and placed a sharp rock inside the rubber band and drew it back. He let it go,

ZING! It went toward the rock and the heron raised his head just as the rock arrived. Down it went dead as a door nail. When J. P. found it and looked at it up close he was not happy about hitting a beautiful creature.

The Creek

J. P. and Jim loved playing in the creek, not just to cool off, but swimming and dunking one another and sometimes fishing, so one day they decided to explore the creek more. Up the creek was a bend that they had never been before. After going around the bend and looking around, there was another bend up the creek. Then there was always another bend to explore. After several bends, they decided they were getting too far from home and turned back. The creek led them, bend after bend, right back home.

Man Decisions

Buck

Growing up on ranch gave twenty-four-year-old Buck had a thorough knowledge of horses. He could ride almost any horse and believed they deserved good care and respect. Wanting to spread his wings beyond the home ranch, he hired on with a dude ranch to guide a bunch of people on rides around the trails and get them back safely. Some the customers wanted the experience but had never climbed in a saddle before this ride. Buck had to look after them as well as the horses.

The dude ranch was popular and usually fully occupied. A swimming pool, tennis courts, and nightly entertainment kept the vacationers happy even if they never got on a horse. Some came for the beauty and serenity of the mountains and valleys to escape a hectic lifestyle for a few days.

Mr. Ray, the owner of the ranch was a nice out-going man who enjoyed conversations with the guests and would often lead one of the trail rides himself. His daughter, just eighteen, thought she was a grown up and had her eye on Buck. When she came around Buck, he sidled away as soon as possible, not wanted to get mixed up with the boss's daughter.

Buck got to know all the horses in the barn as he looked after them and they know him by scent, sound and sight. Leaving them at night well fed and healthy gave him a sense of satisfaction of a good days' work.

His job required him to wear a costume not much different from his usual ranch clothes and hat to give the guests the notion they were in the wild west of bygone years. Out of the top of his boot was dummy rifle, supplied by his employer who thought a real one would make the guests nervous. His only real weapon was a slingshot that rode in his back pocket all the time. He had loved slingshots since he was a boy and liked to shoot at things. When one slingshot wore out, he just made another. Lots of target appeared as he guided the tagalong group around but lots of them were just a leaves or knothole in trees. Killing little animals no one would use for food didn't appeal to Buck unless it was a pest ruining the garden.

One morning he led a string of riders to view the sunrise from a viewing point and coffee stand and then higher up to a camp where another camp provided lunch. From there, an activity director took the quests on a walking trail to view a magnificent waterfall. Buck stayed in camp to feed and water the horses.

income. When he quit his job with no explanation, everybody thinks he has gone crazy.

In his garage, he began to plan how to build a better but simpler grill. The grill the company had was made with two halves of aluminum die cast which was expensive. He decided to make his out of steel which can be bought already cut out in various shapes and sizes by different means. It can be then be formed and welded to become something useful. Steel can also be painted black with a heat resistant paint. His design would be far cheaper to produce than the aluminum die cast one the company produce.

Knowing he could add gas burners later if he wanted, Eden decided to make his grill for charcoal use only. He planned an enclosure in the top with a door like an oven. By using different means he bent the steel and built a prototype that looked good, simple, but he was sure it would work well. He admired his work and felt confident that the heavy duty material he used will last a long time. He moved it outside of the garage for a trial and looked for a bag of charcoal. When the coals were ready he placed a steak on the grill and put a small pan of biscuits in the oven.

Dorthy, the girl who lived down the street came by and saw Eden outside. She had been watching Eden for months and hoping for him to notice her. The sounds from the garage had given her a hint that something was going on but smelling the steak and biscuits gave her an excuse to stop. As she walks up and says, "Hi, Eden, What are you doing?"

Surprised but happy, Eden responded with a smile. "Hey, Dot! You want some steak and biscuits? I just finished making this grill and had to give it a try."

"That sounds great!"

Eden tests the steaks and decides they are cooked to perfection and checks the biscuits. He quickly runs inside to get another paper plate and eating utensils and puts them on an old card table in the garage.

"Why don't we put that outside since the weather is so perfect?" said Dot, reaching with both hands to one side of the table.

"That's a good idea. How about under oak tree in the shade?"

They worked together to bring everything in place with Eden bringing out an old box to sit on and invited her to sit in the only chair. The taste matched the smell and they declared that was the best steak ever. Eden's heart was working overtime at the praise of his success of actually building a grill and cooking food to perfection.

He didn't know if he looked silly smiling all the time but he couldn't help it. The idea of his improved grill and a sharing the food with a pretty girl who readily understood when he explained his design was sheer joy. He looked at her enough to notice she had a good healthy appearance with a shapely body that drew his attention.

Dot also was smiling and interested in every detail. This was an Eden she had not known existed. He had always been good- looking but his shyness had put a damper on conversation. His delight over his design and product showed in the animated way he described the process.

"I really like what you are doing," she said. "I don't have much to do these days so would it be okay with you if I come her and help, maybe a little?"

The smiles just kept coming and Eden quickly accepted her offer. "Yeah! I sure could use some help!" Would wonders never cease Eden thought.

The most of Eden's savings was used to buy the material for about ten grills and sets to work thinking he would see if they would sell. He is confident they are better and cheaper for the customer so he believes the will sell.

Every day Dot arrives and holds the materials steady for him to manipulate into a grill. Sometimes the interfered with conversation but during breaks they discussed their likes and dislikes from food to books to movies. Surprising them, they agreed on most but laughed at the disagreements and the work time flew. Eden discovered that he looked forward to seeing her every day and admired the fact that she could do almost anything. Her biscuits tasted as good as they looked along with whatever meat they decided to grill on his first self-designed grill.

"I'll pay you, Dot, when we sell these. I'm broke right now from buying the materials but that will change in a few days."

"Don't worry about that. I enjoy working here and I am certainly not starving," Dot laughed.

In a few days ten grills were lined up, shiny and beautiful, with an improved design. Eden had calculated the cost per grill, including labor at a fair rate, added about twenty percent for profit and another bit for the cost of selling. The price he decided to assign was about half of the going rate of other grills on market.

Nearby the shopping mall was an area outside where local people sold their homemade wares , anything from honey and jelly to porch swings, so Eden decides that is the logical spot to sell his grills. Together they make some big sign with red lettering saying, "Grill it your way!"

When everything was loaded, Dot asked, "Can I go with you?"

"Sure!" Eden nods his approval and a big grin changes his usually solemn face. "I wanted to ask you to come, but I thought you wouldn't want to sit out there with me all day." He grabbed another folding

"Don't worry about that. I enjoy working here and I am certainly not starving," Dot laughed.

In a few days ten grills were lined up, shiny and beautiful, with an improved design. Eden had calculated the cost per grill, including labor at a fair rate, added about twenty percent for profit and another bit for the cost of selling. The price he decided to assign was about half of the going rate of other grills on market.

Nearby the shopping mall was an area outside where local people sold their homemade wares , anything from honey and jelly to porch swings, so Eden decides that is the logical spot to sell his grills. Together they make some big sign with red lettering saying, "Grill it your way!"

When everything was loaded, Dot asked, "Can I go with you?"

"Sure!" Eden nods his approval and a big grin changes his usually solemn face. "I wanted to ask you to come, but I thought you wouldn't want to sit out there with me all day." He grabbed another folding chair and placed it in the truck. "It may not take all day. I think these will sell quickly." Dot climbed in with the thermos bottle she had brought along with a small cooler of containing a couple of sandwiches and cookies. Her happiness at being including showed in her sparkling eyes.

By near noon, they had everything set up with prices on everything. One grill was cooking hamburgers and sending delicious scents in all directions. Dot had made a grocery run to buy the items needed to sell a few hamburgers and demonstrate the effectiveness of the grill.

By four o'clock, all the grills including the one used for cooking were sold and they had orders for several more. They take a box of money back to the garage and set up the card table and pull up chairs to separate the coins and bills to get an accurate cs mount. Eden noticed Dot was efficient at math and remembered she had been an excellent salesperson to make up for his own reticence. He was good at explaining the benefits of this grill but she added a fun personality to the conversation.

After a successful day, Eden's imaginative mind was running high. If ten made money then he decided that twenty would be the next step. He knew the garage was too small for holding the supplies and having room to work on twenty grills.

A bigger outcome required more floor space and he decided the profit margin should be increased to thirty percent. He went to see the owner of an old empty warehouse down by the railroad tracks. After a strong discussion and long thinking pauses, Eden and the owner decided on a price a little higher than Eden had offered but much lower than the owner had suggested. He knew Eden would pay on time and the empty warehouse had brought in nothing for several months and had no other prospects of a tenant. A long-term agreement between honest men would benefit both of them.

The profit from the sale of the first ten was plenty to buy the supplies for the twenty in his mind. He ordered all metal shell parts already cut to size from the company that had the equipment capable of cutting and shaping. This he knew, from his intense labor on the first grills, would save him time and energy. This time he did the assembly process an easier way, also, completing one operation on all twenty grills then completing the second. The repetitive process proved to be much faster and the same tools were used for

All twenty were on hand before changing to the next operation. Just as he did back when he worked in a factory, he noticed something assembling the first ten grills and adapted a better way of assembling the twenty. Eden's adaptation proved to be quicker and easier, thus producing more product is a shorter time.

When the twenty were finished and Eden loaded up all his truck could transport, he asked Dot to go with him. She was very pleased that Eden was growing in confidence enugh to invite her. She wondered if he would ever tell her he liked her, but she knew it even without words. On the second day, Dot brought some biscuit dough in her cooler and baked them in the enclosure at the top of the grill. After tasting one of her biscuits, the potential customers liked that feature. They worked three days in the afternoon for four hours and sold every grill. They went home with a pile of money after a day's work that seemed like play.

Back in Eden's garage, they put up the card table, sorted and added the coins and dollars and made the calculations of product cost and income. This time there was a lot more profit and Eden knew he could pay Dot and still have investment dollars. Their grill was not only cheaper

and better for the buyer but was easy to sell. Sitting near each other and looking straight into Dot's at close range, Eden saw love and leaned forward until their lips touched. Having never kissed a girl before, Eden was surprised at how wonderful it felt on his lips but also in his heart. Almost as a shock reaction they both stood and Dot reached for Eden and gave him a hardy kiss. That was the spark Eden needed to reach for her and hug her close.

During the night, Eden had a difficult time falling to sleep. He could hardly wait to see Dot again, but his small industry was also fighting for attention. He thought of ideas for expansion. He realizes that if he had a formal company, he would pay more taxes, pay taxes for the employees, match their social security withholdings, and several more things. Many complications arise when a company is dependent on employees and their abilities and willingness to work. By staying as an individual producing something to sell, but too many, he could make a good living with less hassle. It crossed his mind that his little factory was already a two person involvement and he hoped it would be a permanent arrangement.

Before they started in on another twenty, Eden ordered a few more pieces of equipment to make the production easier and quicker.

As they ate under the tree late in the afternoon which had become their custom, Eden looked at Dot so much with a flushed face that she finally asked him, "What is wrong, Eden? You are staring at me."

"Will you marry me?" Eden blurted out.

"Well, that depends on whether you love me or not."

"Yes! Yes! Yes! I love you. I love you so much! So will you marry me?"

"Then I will marry you because I love you very much," Dot added with a tear springing from her eye."

They were not interested in waiting and planning an elaborate wedding, so in a couple of weeks with their parents beaming, the preacher pronounced them man and wife in a small church down the street. On their short wedding trip to the mountains, they enjoyed the views and one another and come home a to a small house they had rented before leaving. They were confident, however, that in a year by working and saving they would be able to buy it.

On the very first morning in their own home, Dot made hot biscuits served with butter and blackberry jelly. It was so good that Eden picked up the jar of jelly and noticed it was homemade.

"Where did you get this jelly? It's even better than what Mama buys." Eden said.

"I always make my own jelly. That is our family way. Actually, this is my grandmother's recipe. I am glad you like it."

"Is it hard to make?"

Dot explained that getting the fruit was sometimes hard but turning it into jelly was not that hard.

"Can you make a bunch of jelly at one time, say enough for twenty jars at once?" Eden continues to inquire.

"I never make just one jar at the time. If I double or triple the recipe, it well be 20 or so jars depending on the size of the jar. Why are you asking all these questions about jelly? I thought your mind was on producing more grills."

Eden explained that this jelly was good enough to put on the market. In fact, it was a shame not to share such goodness , for a profit of course. They came up with a plan, but the flavor would depend on what fruit was in season.

The Man Who Did Not Pay

Harry Burns ran a small dye shop. He is good at his trade and could design almost anything. So, the day he got an order from a man who had a plant that made parts, he was confident he could do it. The order was for Harry to design and build a machine that would save a lot of labor and speed up his production process in his plant.

He delved into the design and soon had a working product ready. The machine was finished, delivered, set up, and began producing the product with precision and speed. Everyone was happy.

Harry's office then prepared the bill for the machine and sent it the man who ordered it. The man refused to pay, claiming it was defective, and he declared he would not pay until it was repaired. Harry went to man's plant, carefully examined the machine found nothing wrong. In fact, it was working and rapidly producing many of the parts just as it was designed to do. Still the man refused to pay for the machine.

That evening Harry simply drove his truck up to back door of the plant and told the workers he needed to take the machine back to his shop to fix it. Someone got a forklift and loaded it on Harry's truck. After he unloaded the machine in his shop, he took parts off and took a cutting torch to the rest, reducing it into scrap steel.

The debtor who refused to pay began calling every day to inquire about the machine. The loss of the machine had ruined his entire operation. Harry continued saying, "I'm working on it." and quickly hung up the phone. In the quiet of his office, his laughter burst out.

Roy and Martha

After Roy's parents died in a car accident, he and a younger brother lived with their aunt. He needed to work from that time on as a teen to have enough money to live on, but not much more.

Since he was determined to get a college education, he looked for job that allowed him to take a few classes every semester. He had two classes at the college in the morning, ate lunch, studied, and rushed to his restaurant job from four to nine every day. He paid his college tuition and still managed to donate money to the family household. Because he wanted his younger brother to have a normal teen life, Roy bought clothes and other stuff for him. He did not date much because he was so busy, plus no money was left for dating. Plenty of girls looked his way, since he was a very good-looking man, but he was careful to be friendly yet keep his distance.

Martha was a young girl twenty-two years old going to college full time because her family had money. They belonged to the local country club and she was popular with everyone at the college.

Martha noticed Roy in biology class and admired the way he looked and acted. Arriving a little early one morning, she stood outside the door until she saw him enter and followed him to seat close to him. She could see he was smart and always asked really sensible questions to the teacher.

One day the class went on a field trip about twenty miles to a small stream. The teacher said, "Pull your shoes and socks off and wade out in the stream and find as many animals or fish you can and make notes about them. Pick out a partner. As soon as you get out put your dry socks and shoes on so you won't get a cold".

Roy looked around to find Martha right beside him, so they became partners. She was a lot of fun, laughing when they always spotted something at the same time. Roy could see she thought a lot like himself. But he thought, "She sure is pretty and I like her, but I don't want her for a date. She is just a rich little girl. We wouldn't have much in common in the ordinary world."

In a few days they were doing another project that required a partner. There was Martha right beside him. Again, they had fun working and produced the best project in the class. It soon became known in the class that Roy and Martha would be partners. Martha knew he was working his way through college and he never asked her for a date, but Martha wished he would. He was better by far than any other boys she knew.

A lady from the city spoke in class one day telling about a contest to demonstrate our city for its $150^{th.}$ birthday. All entries must be complete and turned in within two weeks. The winner will get a reward. Martha turned to Roy and looked him in the eye and he knew what she had in mind. He smiled and shook his head yes. They went into an empty classroom and at a table they began to think of something. They thought just alike, and not just agreeing, it was just like they had the same thoughts. They made a drawing of an old man and woman dressed in straw hats and old clothes in a plowed field. A cat leaned against the woman and a dog stood in the background. Roy put a border around it and put it on a cardboard with string on the back to hang on the wall.

One morning they announced the winners were Roy and Martha. The prize was $500. When Martha heard this, she turned and ran to Roy and grabbed him on both arms with her face close to his. Roy was so excited that he grabbed her into a tight hug. Up close with a beautiful face and love in her eyes, Roy bent down with a tender, gentle kiss that was not real quick. Martha could see love in his eyes as they looked at each other. Roy thought, "What have I done? She is a beautiful young woman, just what I want, but we can't have any future together. I do love her but I wish I didn't."

Someone hollered for Martha to come on and go on the ride with the group. After Martha left, Roy began to face the facts. He decided he had to stop this. I am just a poor boy and she is a rich kid. He thought even if they married and had a child, they would more than likely divorce. What a mess. He decided it was best to stop it right then.

Not wanting to face Martha the next day, Ron stayed home. Martha was so disappointed that Roy wasn't in class or any of the usual places. She knew she loved Roy and they he loved her, too. He had not told her with words but his actions and the look in his eyes spoke to her. She knew their lifestyles were different, but his character and personality were exactly what she wanted in a husband.

That night Martha said, "Dad, may I talk to you about something?"

He said, "Sure let's go out on the front porch".

June said, "Dad, I have fallen in love with a boy at school. I think you will like him, but he doesn't have much money. He is smart, thinks just like me, and I love him."

Martha's dad said," Well, I have always known you to have a good head on your shoulders. If you are satisfied, I am sure it's alright."

Marth said, "He hasn't told me he loves me but I know he does. I could see it in his eyes."

Her dad asked, "What's the problem?"

Martha replied, "He thinks I am a spoiled rich kid, but I'm not."

After Roy missed class two days in a row, Martha went to the college office and got Roy's home address. She then headed to her dad's office and asked him to drive her to Roy's house about ten blocks away. She made him hurry to get there before he went to work.

Roy's aunt answered the door and was surprised to find a beautiful girl asking for Roy.

"Roy, there is someone to see you," his aunt called up the stairs

Roy was even more surprised and quickly stepped out on the front porch and shut the door. He motioned for her to follow him. They go to the end of the porch out of sight of prying eyes.

Martha said straight out, "Roy, I love you very much and I know you love me, too. What's wrong?"

Roy replied, "Martha, you would be making a mistake if we got married. I don't have a cent to court you with, much less marry you. I can't keep up with you, and even if I had money, I wouldn't want to be like the boys at the country club."

Martha said, " I don't want you to be like those boys! We think just alike. We have the same values and life goals. And we have fun! Money can't buy what we have. Will you talk with my dad? He wants to talk to you."

Roy nodded that he would but looked a little nervous.

"He is out in the car." Martha said. "I'll wait here."

Martha's dad saw Roy coming and got out of the car and met him. They shook hands and looked one another over. Martha's dad was dressed in simple clothes and had a kind expression that helped Roy relax. Martha's dad saw a good-looking boy with good manners and liked him from the start. He understood why Martha would be attracted to him.

Martha's dad started the conversation right to the point. "My daughter is very much in love with you and she is pretty sure you love her. Do you?"

"Yes, Sir, I do. But I don't think she would be happy with me for long," Roy answered.

Mr. Adams continued, "She said you don't want her because of her money. Son, I used to be just like you. I didn't always have money. I just got lucky in business and made some money. Martha says you are smart and that you study and work hard. That means that you won't always be poor."

Roy said, "I plan to get a good job as soon as I can but I don't have anything to offer her now. Martha is used to the nicest things and I can't provide that. I don't want her to decide later that life with me is too hard."

"Roy, if you love her and she loves you, things will work out. She has been taught that love is more important than things."

"I believe that, too," said Roy, with hope beginning to rise in his heart.

Her father replied, "Ok, then go get her."

Roy walked up to Martha and took her hand.

"Martha," he said. "Do you want to spend a lot of time with me and see how this goes? I love you but I don't want to rush you into anything."

Martha answered, "I already know how this will go, but, yes, I want to spend time with you! Now take me in and let me meet your aunt in the right way. And I would like to bring my dad in to meet her, too."

"And my brother. Do you know I have a brother?" Roy said realizing that he had never been so happy. Martha thought the exact same thing.

What to Do?

Stan Edwards sat on a bench just outside the hospital staring out and seeing nothing. He just lost his wife and here he sat, 88 years old, and doesn't know what to do. Kingsland Senior Home is a fine place, but he doesn't like it. It isn't home. His thoughts circled but came back to feeling as if he must figure out what to do or he will be put on a shelf waiting to die. He decided he certainly would do something else. He had been on cruises and traveled a lot of places in the world. He could afford to do that kind of thing, but he doesn't want to do any of those things again.

After the funeral he drove home in his Lincoln car and decided that his car was too big. He mulled over buying a small car or an old pick up. He decided to buy an old pickup truck that runs good but did not draw a lot of attention. He wanted to travel around in rural area and observe simple things, like shearing sheep or making molasses.

He told his children what he was going to do and promised to keep in touch by cell phone. He told them to clean out his apartment and keep anything they wanted and sell or give the rest to Goodwill. They questioned what he is doing but agreed to his plan as long as he called one of them daily.

He began to look for a good old pickup truck. Finally, he found one that looked good but the transmission is broken. He bought it cheap because the price to fix the transmission was almost equal to the value of the truck. He got a garage to pick it up and put in a new transmission.

He told the mechanic, "I want it first class condition. Do whatever you need to do."

In about a week he picked it up and took it out for a test. Driving that old truck made him very happy because he loved that old truck. It purred like a kitten and ran smooth. Everything worked and he was ready to go.

He picked out a few clothes and put them in a suitcase he had used for his travels around the world, but this time he took no suits or ties. He loaded a cooler and headed out. He stopped by the bank and got a lot of cash because he planned to only use his credit card if he got in a bind. It was cold enough to turn on the truck heater.

He noticed a farm where workers were preparing to butcher some hogs and he decided to stop and watch. People kill hogs when it gets cold enough to preserve the meat in an unheated building. Several people stood around and he joined them but felt he stood out like a sore thumb. He told them he just wanted to watch, that he didn't know anybody and promised he would stay out of the way.

They had a huge homemade tub made with wood and a metal bottom set up about a foot off the ground with rocks and dirt piled up by the side. A big fire burned under the pan that is full of hot water. One of the men shot the hog in the head and another cut its throat to bleed the body free of blood. They dipped the hog in the hot water to loosen the hair on the hog. It took four men to hang it up from a strong tree limb by its hind legs, scrape off the hair, cut it down the middle and took out all of its internals. They dismembered it and took all the parts to large homemade worktables where several women worked. The feet, head, ears, liver, shoulders, hams, sides, back, and bottom parts had be trimmed of excess fat, cleaned, and prepared for curing process. Two cast iron skillets with fire underneath cooked the fat to render the lard.

Everybody worked and looked forward to something good to eat. Happy time. As he left, Stan thought about the joy he felt. He also knew he needed to buy some clothes and shed his city slicker look.

Stan stuck to the back roads and took his time. As he is traveled along, a creek with tree limbs hanging over the shallow water caught his attention. What a beautiful sight he thought. He pulled over and went down by the creek bank and sat down. It was so peaceful. "Yeah," Stan said to himself. "This is way yonder better than the senior home."

A few more miles down the road, he stopped at a country store and looked around. In the back they sold fried chicken, so he bought some. He noticed that the motels along this route were simple, but good enough for him to rest. He took his time getting up and was in no hurry to leave.

A man near the motel was making chairs outside his little house. Stan went over and watched him and asked questions. The man was glad to show him around and answer questions. When he left, he had bought a chair that he didn't need and put it in the back of the truck.

The next day he came up on a lot of cars parked beside of the road and saw a farm auction in process. He thought this would be interesting, so he found a parking spot. He didn't need to check in because he didn't intend to buy anything. Besides, he didn't want to be tempted to bid on something. The house items went first , then the farm equipment, and then the house and land. It was interesting to watch people.

The day is getting late and he noticed that he was short on cash. He checked in at a motel and slept late so he could go to a bank and try to get some cash. At the bank he asked for a bank officer and explained he would like to write a check for about two thousand and get electronic approval. He is told the bank would do it but it will take another day. Stan agreed and planned to stay over another night. Stan had an urge to go to the bathroom and he asked the bank officer if he could us their bathroom. It was a bathroom for employees only, but he was given permission. While sitting on the commode, in a stall with the door shut, two men come in talking.

One said, " You know, it looks like you are going to get that farm you want. Her note is due this week and I know she has no way of paying."

"Are you going to extend the note?" the other man asks.

Stan decided the first man must be the president and heard him say "No."

Stan sat there for a while because he does not want them to know he heard. As he was leaving the bank, he looked in the president's office to see what he looked like. The next day when he was in the bank, an old lady came in and went into the president's office. He could see she was pleading for him to extend the loan. He could also see the answer was no.

As she was leaving, Stan decided to follow her home to see where she lived. It was a nice old farm but a little run down. He thought, "I have plenty of money and I don't want to see her hurt. I'm going to help her if I can."

He went up and knocked on her door. She came to the door and said, " I don't need anything."

He said, "Mam, I'm not a salesman. I just want to talk to you a few minutes."

She asked, " What about?"

He said, "Your farm."

She said, "Well, come on in."

As they sat down, he explained, " My name is Stan Edwards. I was in the bank yesterday when I overheard two men talking. They don't know I heard. They plan on taking your farm. I don't like that and I have a lot of money and I want to help you."

She says, "Could you do that?"

He said, "Yeah".

She told him she owed a fifteen-hundred-dollar payment and the total payoff was about three thousand. Stan told her that tomorrow he was supposed to be getting two thousand in cash and that he will give you enough to make a payment.

"After you make the payment" Stan said, "We will decide what to do about paying it all off."

She said, "Oh, that is so good! Thank you, Thank you!"

She found out Stan was staying at a motel and said, "Will you stay for supper?"

He said, "I sure will, thank you."

She said, " You just sit down there while I will fix something."

Stan sat in an old straight chair and waited. Soon he was served good coffee, fried country bacon, and eggs with a warmed oven biscuit. It hit the spot. Before he left, he took the chair from the back of his truck and gave it to her. She was so glad.

The next day he went into the bank and got the three thousand in cash. That afternoon he picked her up at her farm and drove her to the bank. After giving her the cash, he asked ,"Would you like me to go in with you?"

She answered, "Yes."

They went in and sat down at the bank officer's desk. She was a lady, but not the same one I talked to earlier.

She said, "How are you Mrs. Wright?"

Mrs. Wright answered, "I would like to make a payment on my loan."

The officer studders not expecting that. She left her desk and said, "I will be right back in a few minutes. Here comes a man to take over."

Stan expects it to be the man he had overheard. Mrs. Wright said again, "I want to make a payment on my loan." She dug in her old pocketbook and pulled out a roll of one-hundred dollar bills.

The man said, "Where did you get that?"

Then Stan spoke, "Sir, that doesn't matter, and it is none of your business. Just give us a receipt."

As we left, Mrs. Wright was all smiles. She said, "If you will stop by a grocery store and buy chicken, I will make supper."

Supper that night was fried chicken, hot biscuits, milk gravy, mashed potatoes, home canned green beans and, of course, good coffee. After supper we sat and talked about things. She enjoyed her new chair. He hated to go to the motel, but he thought he should.

The next day he went over to the farm and she showed him from the window of the pick-up truck. The farm had a lot of tall grass because she did not have livestock. On the back side of the farm there was a creek that ran water year around, an ideal place to raise stock. He told her if she had about ten calves they would grow on this grass and water. He suggested that he loan her enough money to buy you some calves and pay off her debt. The loan would be with low interest and long term. She is really happy to agree to that. She said she had a friend that would help her buy the calves.

That afternoon Stan went into town and into another bank. He thought he had used up his welcome at the other. He got the bank to arrange to give him five thousand dollars after it is approved by electronic mail. He spent the rest of the afternoon walking around the town. It was a nice little town and everybody seemed friendly.

The next day he got the money, picked up Mrs. Wright and went to the bank. He had made out a note for her to sign. After she signed the note Stan gave her four thousand dollars that was enough to buy some calves and pay off the farm loan. They went into the bank and over to the officer's desk. The other man came over to see what they want. He did not say a single word but he just stood there with no greeting.

Mrs. Wright says," I want to pay off my loan."

He still did not say a word, but he motioned for the bank officer to go ahead. Steve said, "We would like to have the note marked, 'paid in full'." They paid and left with the note in hand. He took her out to eat and then home. She told him she was very blessed by him and declared that she would write and tell him about the farm doings.

Back at the motel he read a little. hunkered down, and slept soundly until and he heard rooster crowing. He wanted to say goodbye to the old man, so he got up and found something to eat in his cooler. He loaded his things in the truck and saw the old man up and moving around. The old man is pleased and friendly and thanked him again.

Stan decided to get back on the interstate highway for a few miles. He passed through hills country until he stopped for get his gas tank full and oil checked. There was a Goodwill store so he went in and looked around and found exactly what he needed in the men's department. An old pair of overalls, faded and worn, was just his size. He bought an old flannel shirt and thinks he will blend in with a lot of rural folks. He asked if he could use their restroom and then left the store wearing what he had just bought.

Further on down the old two-lane road he came to a little town with just a few buildings. There was no fast food in the town so he went in a family restaurant that specialized in fried catfish so he ordered the special. As he is ate he noticed people not getting waited on and a big sign in the window saying, "Help Wanted."

Stan called the man over to his table and said," Look, I am just traveling around with nothing to do. If you want me to, I can cook, wash dishes, wait on tables for a few days."

He looked Stan over and said," I don't pay much."

Steve replied, "That's okay as long as I can get room and board."

He said," Okay, come with me."

Next door, there was a building that had an office out front for a motel and a back room with a water heater and stuff. The man said, "If I put a bed in here, will it be alright?"

Stan said, "Yeah, that's fine but I don't want to work more than eight hours a day." The man said, "That's ok."

The man took him to the kitchen and showed him where everything was and the procedure for filling orders.

He got a big white apron and a white hat. He was told to cook first and it was fun. He cooked hamburgers, bacon, and eggs, things like that. There was an old chair in the back that he used when he wasn't busy. He saw the dishes needed washing so he washed the dishes. When the man that ran the restaurant came in, he saw Stan washing dishes and everything running smooth. He was really pleased and said, "You eat anything you want back here."

Stan said ok. They closed at nine and the man showed Stan the bed he had moved in. It was ok. He said, "If you work from 8 to 4, would that be ok?"

Stan said, "Ok, just right." That night he slept good, just as good as in a motel.

The next morning at eight Steve was ready to go. There was a bathroom he could use. He had a shower and felt good. He knew how to cook an egg over easy without bursting the yellow. He stayed busy most of the morning, cooking breakfast for everybody. He helped make out a menu. He put a few things in the menu he knew how to do, like creamed potatoes with onion. It was potatoes well cooked, whipped with a mixer, with chopped onions, and graded cheese. Everybody liked it. He felt good.

In the afternoon at four, he walked around the town in all the stores. People got to know him as the cook. His boss let him go to church on Sunday. It was old time singing and he enjoyed it. People got to know him and treated him friendly. Some of the people needed help but they did not want to accept anything free. That's just the way they were.

After five days the boss was able to hire someone and he was ready to hit the road again. The boss thanked him and offered him some money. but he said no. He had done a good job.

Stan traveled down the old two lane road about twenty miles and noticed a car c behind him with sirens blowing and blue lights flashing. He thought, "What have I done to cause all this?"

When he looked out his window there was a big fat man with a badge on his shirt. He was pointing a pistol at him and said, "Step out of the truck and keep your hands where I can see them."

When Stan got out he was slammed up against the truck and put into handcuffs.

Stan asked, "Whats wrong? What have I done?"

The sheriff said, "You are under arrest for stealing."

Stan was taken to the county seat and put in jail. They had his truck towed in and put in a lot. Nobody would talk to him and he spent the night in jail.

The next morning some farmers came in and looked at him. One of them said. " Why that's the cook at Joe's place! That's not the man we are looking for."

Stan was cleared of all wrongdoing. They were looking for a man that had stolen a calf and butchered it. The sheriff took him to his truck and apologized for his rough treatment. Stan was sure glad that was over.

He decided to go through Gatlinburg on the way east. He stopped in town and got a motel. He took a good tub bath, changed his clothes into dress clothes, and then took a walk through town looking at everything and everybody. He left town the next morning, going up over the mountain.

He is enjoyed the drive and though this is much better than the senior home. He checked in with his children and everything is ok. In a little while he got off the tourist roads and headed southeast on a small paved road. The area was a lot different with not many houses. He soon came to a little river running beside the road and noticed hunters camped beside the river.

Stan pulled in at one of the camps and said, "How you doing? You getting anything?"

They are friendly and said, "Not yet."

One says, "You want some coffee?"

Stan thanked him and sat down by their fire on the ground and enjoyed some conversation with them. When he left he thinks, "I couldn't do this at the senior home."

He was glad he to be free to do whatever he wants. It began to get dark and there are no motels anywhere. He was afraid to just park just anywhere, so he drove on until he finally he saw a church and he decided to park in its parking lot.

He stretched out on his seat and was soon fast asleep. Lights flashing in on him around nine woke him up. The man outside with a flashlight saw Stan said, "Mr. are you alright?"

Stan sat up, opened the door and said, "I am alright, I just got tired and did not have anywhere to stay, so I thought I would take a nap in a church parking lot."

The man replied, " That's ok, but why don't you come on in the church? It's a better place to sleep."

Stan said, "Ok, I will. Thank you."

He took him to the church and said, " You can sleep here by the stove. It's going out but it will take awhile."

Stan says, "That's real good, thank you."

He stretched out by an old pot belly stove and the heat felt real nice.

The man hollers as he is leaving, "See you in the morning."

There was a small light on at the door. Stan is really thankful of his good fortune and it do not take very long for him to go to sleep.

People talking woke him up the next morning. Stan and went into the room where he man he saw last night and four other men were about to have a breakfast meeting in the kitchen. It turned out the man last night was the preacher and the others were deacons. One man was cooking breakfast. Steve is asked to stay. Stan sat at a table with them. The cook brought out the breakfast of eggs, bacon, and biscuits. There was a coffee cup at each place and a pot of coffee was passed around. The preacher asked the Lord's blessing. The good breakfast hit the spot with Stan.

One of the men said, "We are going to have a deacon's meeting here at the table. You can stay if you want to."

Stan said, "Thank you, I think I will stay."

At the meeting they talk about everything in the church. Stan just listened. Finally, they began to talk about a family that was having trouble. The man in the family had to go to the hospital and has not been able to work for a long time and he is the bread winner for the family. They had run out of food, money, and everything. The church didn't not have much money to help them.

Stan thought of his own money and wanted to help. He raised his hand up. Stan said, "I am going to make a donation to the church for twenty-five hundred dollars to take care of that family. Use the rest as you see fit."

The man said, "Really? That is so good! Thank you and may God bless you!"

Stan said, "Don't tell them where the money came from."

That night Steve built a fire in the stove and slept good. He felt good too. It is more blessed to give than to receive. The next morning he headed out wondering what he would run into next. He looked forward to getting to the beach.

That evening walked down about two blocks from his motel to get a fish dinner. After eating he decided to walk back up a street parallel to the beach road. It had no cars or people and was peaceful. Beside the road another motel was under construction with a tall plank fence all around it. When he got to it, there are four men coming from the opposite direction.

When they meet one of the men said, "Hi bud, where are you from?"

At the same time he stuck his hand out and said, " My name is Joe, what's yours?' He had Stan's hand in a tight grip. One of the other men grabbed his left hand and said, "My name is Joe, too."

They press him up against the fence and one said, " Can you give us some money to eat on?"

Stan said, "I don't have much money. You can have whatever I got. Just leave me alone."

One of the others pulled his wallet out of his back pocket and said, "How much you got?"

Stan said, "I think a twenty and some ones."

The man with the pocket book said, "He is right but here are some credit cards." As they look at the credit cards and one man said, "The Walgreen and Kroger are not credit cards. They are no good."

One stuck the cards into Stan's front pocket and landed a fist in his stomach. Stan had seen it coming and tightened his stomach. It did not hurt him that bad but he made out like it did. He bent over and slid down the fence to a sitting position. He shut his eyes like he was hurting bad, but he could still see. He studied their faces. They left him there.

After they left Stan thought that was sure a bunch of dumb guys. He had a hundred-dollar bill in a zipper pocket in his wallet and cell phone in his front pocket.

He got out his cell phone and called 911 and reported his location. In a few minutes a police car pulled up. They took him to a clinic for a check-up. Stan objected but they said they have to. He thought that was going to be an easy case for the police. The clinic said he was fine and the police took him to the motel. Stan wondered, "What is going to happen tome next. It looks like something always does. Maybe I better go back home for awhile."

That night in bed Stan lay thinking, "I miss my children and they probably miss me too. I need to go home."

The next morning his mind was made up. He was going home. He called the airline and bought a ticket for the next day. Then he called his children for someone to meet him at the airport. That gave him one day to sell the truck. He sold the truck to a car dealer and threw in the cooler. The next day he took a cab to the airport. When he arrived at his home airport, he was surprised. There are all four of his children waiting for him. They hugged each other and were so happy to see him. On the way home, they all stopped to eat out and talk.

One of his sons said, "Dad, I have an idea. Me and Thelma have talked it over. We would like for you to come live with us. We could build an extra bedroom with bath on the end of our house. You can help me build it. You can come and go whenever you like."

Stan thought awhile and said, "That sounds good but are you sure you want me? I don't want to hinder you."

The son said, "Dad, we love you and want you." Stan said, "Ok."

Something

Worthwhile

Chapter 1

I crawled out of bed and left for work by six thirty in the morning as usual with no idea that today was the beginning of a new life. As I drove to work feeling fine after a good hot cup of coffee and expected the sun to keep on shining, but, for some reason unknown to me, my mind kept reviewing my situation. I liked my job and I was good at it. Hopefully, the raises would continue to come on a regular basis. I was satisfied at being twenty-three years old and had already completed my apprenticeship in tool and die making so my job was secure.

My boss was tough sometimes, but I had no problem with that since he was fair and only expected quality work. Just as I got to our shop, nudged my way past everybody crowded around the time clock, and punched in with a minute to spare, my boss hollered, "Hey, Lloyd! Are you working on that *&*&*&* die?"

"Yep, that's an easy job. I'll be finished sometime today." Sometimes, I got a progressive die job and which is much harder, but I liked the challenge.

At nine thirty, the break bell rang and we got a ten minute break, releasing the ones of us who hadn't brought a sandwich from home to rush across the street to a small grocery store. Two or three of my buddies liked to get a bologna sandwich and look at the owner's daughter who waited on us when she had a day off school. She seemed to smile at me a little more and usually asked me if I had seen the latest movie. I thought about asking her out, but she was just a senior in high school, and I was already a grown man. I was holding off until her graduation and she would be almost as grown-up as me. I hoped nobody got her to go steady before then, but Mama had always said not to date girls much younger than me and I had been careful about that.

As we paid, some of the guys bought lottery tickets so I bought one, too. I don't know why as I usually didn't. The chances of winning were next to nothing.

A few days later, when I went in to work someone hollered, "Lloyd, the winning lottery ticket was sold across the street! Where's your ticket?"

"I don't know, maybe in my toolbox." I didn't remember putting it in my wallet so I began digging in my toolbox and moving wrenches out of the way, It was there but oil soaked from my oil can leaking from with a loose lid. That was unusual as I was particular about my tools but sometimes other guys borrowed my things. I could make out the numbers and we compared them with the numbers one of the guys had written down from the early trip to the little grocery before work. They matched!

Winning the lottery didn't seem possible, so I rechecked and the guys checked and it was plain to see that I had the winning, though oil soaked, ticket. I wondered if it would be valid. I was dumbfounded and rushed across the street to check with the grocery store owner. He checked and assured me that the numbers matched, and he would call the authorities to see what I should do.

I am so dumbfounded that I went back to work not knowing what else to do. But my concentration was on winning the lottery, therefore, designing a tool was beyond my ability. Finally, I asked my boss for the day off. He agreed, knowing my body was willing to work but my mind was whirling about seemingly impossible things.

The grocery story owner reported to the lottery authorities who advised me to bring it to an office in the city. I could hardly believe it when I walked out with a check, a big check, and made my way to bank. I asked for privacy, not wanting a bunch of people demanding part of it before I even got to think about what to do. The newspaper made a few pictures, but I pulled my hat down low hoping no one would identify me. The newspaper honored my request to use my initials and only a few details about me, saying I was a working man.

All the way home my mind jumped from possibility to possibility. How much would it be? It seemed I should get organized, so as soon as I entered my door I went straight to the drawer and pulled out a tablet and began to write down the possible expenses I already knew were ahead. Right then, I had enough money to live on with the salary I brought in now. I thought I would need more if I got married and bought a house. But that wouldn't be much of twenty million! The number twenty million was in my head, but was that real? Maybe it was twenty thousand. Even if it was twenty million the government would take half in taxes and that would only leave ten million.

Only ten million??? I thought I had lost my mind. That was still more than I would need for the rest of my life, so I didn't need my job anymore, but what on earth would I do? I didn't want to do nothing for the rest of my life so I needed more time to think. I decided to take one day at a time and not do any foolish throwing around money .

Chapter 2

After the lottery money actually came through to the bank, the IRS took about half and the other half stayed, deposited temporarily in the local bank. My family and community were happy to help me with ideas of how use my new wealth. The girl at the grocery store graduated from high school and accepted my invitation to the movie. She was very happy for me and insisted I drive through upscale neighborhoods to see what magnificent houses were for sale.

It soon became apparent that even twenty million would not last long if I took all the suggestions coming from friends and strangers. A vacation seemed a good plan to get away from the pressure of people chasing after me wanting a donation or trying to sell me something. I decided to buy an old truck. I had already had to quit work because the guys there didn't treat me the same anymore. Some teased with serious intent that I should share a few million with them and some were so jealous they wouldn't even speak. I wanted to work but the boss encouraged me to get out of the way, so I did.

The old truck I found suited me just fine. I had prayed for God to guide me in making decisions even about buying the truck. It ran good so I was confident it would take me wherever I needed to go.

A few more things needed to be taken care of before I could leave with a free conscience, including ending things with Clara who seemed to think we would marry. I liked her and she was prettyas a picture, but I didn't love her. I pulled up at the store and she came running out and jumped in on the passenger side with a puzzled look on her face. She reached for my hand and exploded. "Lloyd, I've been watching for you! I thought you were getting a new truck or a Thunderbird. What are you doing in this old truck?"

"Clara, I need to explain a few things. I am sorry to disappoint you, but I don't want a new vehicle of any kind, at least right now. There are important decisions I have to make so I am going on a vacation to see things and make a plan."

"But Lloyd, we can elope. and you would have me along with you! I know you love me!"

"That might work if we loved each other, but we don't. I know you had your eyes on Thomas before I won the lottery. You are really pretty and fun and I like you, but I don't love you as a man should love a wife. Here's a little present to remember our fun times, but I hope you and Thomas will have a really happy marriage."

I gave her a gold bracelet with the word 'Friend' engraved on it and kiss on the cheek. Clara's eyes looked a little damp, but I knew she wasn't broken hearted and I was free to go.

I took my phone off the hook. At church, one of the deacons cornered me and asked me to pay off the church mortgage , but I'm not going to do it. Being a Christian requires everybody to give something. I agreed to send a check for a few hundred dollars, but the entire mortgage was not my obligation.

It became clear I needed to go somewhere quick, so I stopped at the travel office on the way home and there was a tour bus leaving in the morning to go out west. I paid cash and signed up. I changed my last name from Brown to Black for the trip. In leaving day I took a small bag and rode the city bus downtown to the bus station. I got on the tour bus and we traveled miles and miles. I began to meet people and talk about just anything. Nobody recognized me and that was good. I acted tight with my money and let everybody know that I was a tool and die maker. We went to the Grand Canyon and all the tourist places. It was good for about two days, but I knew I was not solving my problem .

When I got home I picked up a stack of my mail. It took a long time to sort out and read some of it and throw away the rest. I went by my shop and took a fifty dollars gift cards for a nice restaurant for everybody . They all wanted to know what I was going to do. I told them I didn't know yet, but it wouldn't be something silly.

Chapter 3

As I went home I stopped at a used car parking lot to look for a used pickup truck. I saw a ten-year-old GMC truck that looked good. It had seventy thousand miles on it, but the engine ran good, the brakes worked fine and the air conditioning was OK. I went home and kept it on my mind all night. I decided that I really wanted to do it.

The next morning I went down and traded my car for it. Then I went to a car shop and had it serviced and new tires put on. The next morning I was ready to go and I headed south with my cooler and my suitcase. I didn't know where I was going but I headed south on I-65.

I got off the Interstate in Georgia and I was on two lane road heading South. I realized it was getting late and I was hungry, but I didn't see my any motels in this rural area. I saw a store with a restaurant, pulled in and ordered coffee and a hamburger with fries. Nobody else was in the restaurant and it was really quiet until a young couple came in with the two small children. As I sipped my coffee, I watched the hardworking young man taking his children out for a treat. I could see the children were very hungry and they had on warn and ragged clothes. They needed new shoes, too. I went to pay the cashier who was a pretty young lady about two or three years younger than me .

She rang up my bill and I said, " See that couple back there with kids? I want to pay their bill."

Nothing was said for a short while. I said, "Don't tell them who paid, just somebody."

She smiled and said, "That's mighty nice of you. They need it."

I said, " Can you tell me where I can find a motel?"

She told the nearest one is in Albany about forty miles on down the road.

I didn't want to drive forty more miles today so I said, "I've been traveling all day and I'm tired. Would it be alright if I took a long nap in my car in your parking lot?".

She said, "I guess so. I will tell my boss so he will know. Thank you. You are nice."

She smiled. She hesitated a while and then said, " See that church across the street? In about 30 minutes they're going to have a social. You're welcome to come if you want to."

Before I answered I asked, "Will you be there?

She looked at me and smiled while shaking her head yes.

"By the way, my name is Lloyd Brown. What's yours?"

She said, " June. I may go for a little while."

While I got back to my truck I sat and thought about the girl. I believed she was glad I asked if she was going to be there. I liked her. I decided to go.

When I got to the entance door of the church but it was a little dark because of a burnt out light bulb. I went inside to light that was so bright I could hardly see. I stood there while my vision began to return. Here came June with another girl.

She said, "Mr. Brown I'm glad you came. I would like for you to meet a few people."

She took me to a table and introduced me to the pastor, her brother, and her sister and her husband. We talked and drank punch, but I kept looking at June. Her brother had a small machine shop and when he found out I was a tool and die maker, we had a lot in common. I found out she was going to college and she was at home on break from a college about forty miles away at Albany.

She took me around to other tables. She and her girlfriend introduced me to a lot of people. I felt flattered.

After a while I told her, "I'm tired and need to get a little sleep."

She walked me to the door and I realized I was holding her hand. As I left I said, "I had a really good time and I hope I will see you again sometime."

I woke up to up to daylight so I headed south keeping on the back roads. When I got to the Gulf Coast, I walked the beach and enjoyed the beauty of the ocean. In the late afternoon I went to a nice restaurant and realized I had plenty money to eat wherever and whatever I wanted. As I ate, I realized I could not get that girl out of my mind. I wondered what she would say if I told her I had money . She was smart, pretty, had good manners, and was a Christian. I liked her family, too. She might be the girl I would like to marry. I needed to see her again.

I called the college and got her phone number. A strange voice answered and I found out it was a common phone for several people.

While I waited, holding the line, someone found her and she answered. I said, "This is Lloyd Brown. How are you?"

She said, "I'm OK. Is something wrong?"

I said. "No, I just want to see you again. Can I come see you next weekend?"

We decided to meet about noon Saturday. I got to town before noon because I had to find the college. I drove around the campus and stopped at the library and called her and told her was in front of the library. In a few minutes here she came with a nice swift gait. I got out of my truck and grabbed her hands. She seemed pleased to see me.

I said, " You look pretty."

She blushed as thanked me. I saw a bench in front of the library and I pointed to it and she we sat down.

"Do you know something we can do together? I asked.

"Well, there is a carnival coming to the college this afternoon about two o'clock. That sounds like it might be fun."

"OK, let's drive around town and you can show me and we will stop and get some coffee or something." We stopped at a place near the college where a lot of the students hung out. We had coffee and donuts. Two students waved at her as she sat down and I could see people thought a lot of her.

The carnival had rides and games and silly stuff. We stopped at a ride of little cars that ran around and round with people bumping into it one another. We got into one car and began to ride around. The other drivers started bumping into us, with everybody laughing. We started bumping into some of them who bumped us. Everybody had fun. I liked the way she laughed. We rode the ferris wheel and some other things until it was time to say goodbye. She had some studying she had to do at five o'clock. I asked for her address and she said she would answer if I wrote first.

We looked at each other for a few seconds and I said. "I like you a lot."

She smiled and said, "Well, I like you too."

I leaned forward and gave her a quick little kiss.

Chapter 4

I decided not to go back to the beach but to just head home. I had some decisions to make. I visited my mother and dad and then my sister. During our talk, I found out my sister and her husband were donating some money to an Indian school in Wyoming.. I got home and I began to think. I had money and no obligations at home, so I thought why don't I fly up there, rent a car, and check it out. I might want to donate a little to it, besides, it would be fun.

I bought a plane ticket to Ashley, Wyoming, and reserved a car. I called ahead for someone to meet me at the school. I drove about an hour to the school. The lady who met me had worn and faded clothes, but they were still good. Her desk was in the corner of a classroom and it was still being used.

She said, "Have a seat. Class will be over in a few minutes. Then I can talk to you."

I said, " OK." That was good. It gave me a chance to see the children. They were well behaved and seemed anxious to learn. When the children left, she came over and sat down at her table. The table was her desk. I could see she was using cardboard boxes for a filing cabinet. She looked at me as though she did not know what to think of me. I don't look like I'm a big donor.

She said, "What can I do for you?"

"I've been traveling around a little and my sister and her husband have donated to the school," I answered. "I told my sister I would look at the school for her and see how things are going."

She said, "That's wonderful! I'm glad to show you around. Ask me anything."

As we were walked around outside, I saw several buildings. One was a dining room building with a kitchen. I noticed a trailer with a large plastic water tank beside the back door and two outhouses. I guessed one was for boys and the other was for girls. I saw two boys behind one of the outhouses peeing. I didn't blame him.

She said, "We run mostly on donations. Some people donate used clothing or food boxes. There's a great need here. Some of these children were just abandoned by their parents. Alcohol and drugs are mostly to blame, but some have no job and no skills so they just give up."

We went into the dining room and found big long picnic tables with bench seats. Children were standing around outside.

She continued to explain, "The kids are getting ready to eat. See that little boy and girl over there? They're new here. The little girl is the boy's sister. They were passed around to relatives for a while. They were so happy when we gave them a new pair of shoes and something to eat."

I thanked her for showing me around and left for town. I had told her I would let my sister know what I had seen.

Chapter 5

As I was drove back to my motel, I continued to
think of what a lot of problems they had. They had to haul
water and I didn't see how they could survive much longer. I
took a bath and cleaned up, put on better clothes, and went
out to eat. I saw an Arby's down the street and since I liked
their chili, I decided to just walk there. I ate and thought
about the school, wondering what I would do if I were in
charge. I don't know, maybe give up, but there are the
children. What would happen to them?

I went back to the motel and turned on the TV, got a
movie on and tried to forget the school. The next morning as
I ate breakfast, I tried to think what I would do until twelve
o'clock when I would catch my plane. I decided to just drive
around in the rural area.

A few miles out of town, I saw a small ranch with a
small barn with a windmill. A windmill! He had windmill
with a well. I pulled over and noticed some one sitting out
on the front porch. I drove in and introduced myself. His
name was Mr. Webster. He was in his eighties and seemed

pleased to talk to someone. He said his well was dug about ten years ago because it was needed for the dry season. I saw two or three cows and some chickens. I found out that in the early spring it rains and the grass grows and in the dry season it dries up. It is still good food for stock and wild animals, but the animals have to have drinking water.

Mr. Webster liked to talk so I just sat there and listened. His wife had died a few years ago and he lived by himself. I enjoyed listening to him.

When I left he said "You come back and see me."

I said I would and wondered if I really would be come back someday. As I was drove back to the airport I thought, "That school needs a well to supply water all the year. I saw lights in the dining room. If they have electricity, they could have an electric pump."

Back home I told my sister the whole story. I had not heard from June. I am afraid she had got the message that I don't want her since I had not called her from out west. After fooling around for a day or two doing nothing I knew I had to do something. Maybe digging a well for that school was something worth doing. I needed to research the possibility. I needed June. I must love her since I thought about her all the time. I didn't know if she would have me and I didn't know what she would think about my money. I needed to see her again. I called about five o'clock the next day when I knew she would be out of class for the day.

I said, "June, this is Lloyd. I need to see you again. . I think about you all the time. I must be in love."

She said, "Yeah. When do you want to come ?"

"How about five o'clock in front of the library the day after tomorrow?"

She said, "OK, I'll be there. See you then."

The drive down had no traffic problems, so I got to the college early . I sat and waited. I was nervous about what she would say. She came walking fast with a big smile on her face. I grabbed her and kissed her. She responded with a tender kiss of her own. We stepped back and looked at each other.

I said. " I love you."

She said, "I know. I love you, too!"

We walked to my car with our arms around each other. I said, "I have some things to tell you. First, I'm twenty-three years old in good health. I'm a journeyman tool and die maker and I'm good at it. I'm a Christian and I want to marry you if you will have me."

She said, "I will. Yes."

I said, "You may not want to after I tell you something."

"What's that?" she asked with fear in her eyes.

"I won the lottery. I've got a lot of money."

After a while she said, "Everybody's going to say I married you for your money and you may think that too!"

I said, "Now the fact that I love you and I know you love me nothing, else matters."

We just sat in the car and talked. I told her what I have been doing and she listened with astonishment. We agreed that we would visit her parents on her next school break. I kept kissing her. What a great feeling to love someone who loves you, too. We decided to wait until next year when she finished college to get married. I returned home in good spirits and visited my sister and told her everything.

Chapter 6

I needed to see if a well could be dug at the school,
how much it would cost, and who would do it. The best way
to do this was to go talk with Mr. Webster again. I flew out
there, rented a car, and drove out to his ranch.

When I pulled in his drive I saw him down at his
barn. He recognized me when I climbed out of the car and
said, "How are you doing?"

I told him I was fine and explained that I needed to
talk to him some more.

He said, "Well, let's go up to the porch and set
down."

I don't want people to know I'm interested in digging
a well at the school until it's for certain. I ask him politely
how he is but he wants to get to point.

He said, "OK, what do you want to talk about?"

I said, " I may be interested in digging a well and I
know you could tell me a few things."

He said, "OK, shoot."

I said, "How did you know where to dig?"

"My well digger told me. I knowed him for a long time. He used a divinin' stick but I believe he just used good common sense." He looked up and grinned.

"Or is just plain lucky."

I asked. "Is it easy to find water around here?"

He said, "I don't know but I might."

"If you do, I hope you use my man. He knows his business. He's the man you need to see. I know where he's working and he comes home about every night to his place about seven or eight miles from here. He finds water most of the time but it's still a gamble."

I told Mr. Webster I would like to see his digger and Mr. Webster promised to call him tonight and see when they could meet. He volunteered to go with me if I wanted him to and I told him I would appreciate that since I didn't know a thing about well digging.

We went out the next day late in the evening and he introduced me to Bob Webster. I was surprised and I looked at the old man. He grinned, "First cousins." He had not told me he was kin to him on purpose. He liked to joke. The well digger, Mr. Webster was old too, but not quite as old and the first Mr. Webster and was lean, all muscle and suntanned.

The next morning I followed him out to his rig to watch him dig. I wore work clothes and helped him unload some supplies. It looked like a good rig. I had an understanding of machines so I enjoyed seeing how this one worked.

At noon he stopped to eat a sandwich I had a chance to talk to him. "Mr. Webster, I may be interested in digging a well. Can you go with me to a place and see if you think we can find water there?"

He said, "How far away is the place?"

I explained, "It was at least a half day's drive or a little more. The place is home of a bunch of orphan kids. It has no running water and the kids need help."

He thought awhile he said, "How about Saturday?"

I picked him up on Saturday about eight o'clock and headed for the school. I didn't want him to know I was the one paying for the work so I told him I represented somebody interested. We met the lady that I met on my first trip but I forgot her name. I remembered it was an Indian name.

I called her aside and said, "I represent someone interested in knowing if water can be found on the school grounds. But don't get your hopes up. We're just checking."

She nodded her head and I left the new Mr. Webster to look around on his own. Finally, he pointed at a spot and said, "If it was mine, this is where I would dig."

I asked, "Do you see any problems?"

He said, "No, but I don't know for sure or how deep I will have to dig."

He gave me a rough idea of the cost. After I took him back home, I headed for the airport. I wanted to talk this over June and see what she thought. I wanted her to be part of what I do.

Thoughts about the well filled my head. If they dug a well and find water, they would need lots of plumbing for bathrooms, showers, and kitchen sinks. But first things first. Don't count your chickens before they hatch I remembered.

Chapter 7

Whoever I donated to I wanted most of it to go directly to the cause, not some fat salaries and miscellaneous stuff. I needed to get June to go with me into the school, plus check the cost etc. Whatever I did, I wanted her to be involved and I didn't want her to approve just to please me. I was anxious to go home with June. I hope they liked me. The next break was in two weeks. I had a hard time waiting.

I got on the phone headed for Albany to meet June. I rented a car and we drove to her home. When I met her she looked so good I could not keep my hands off her. I pulled close and I kissed her.

As we were drove down the two-lane road, we were both quiet, just thrilled to be together. She said, "I made the honor roll."

I said, "That's good! I knew you were smart. Have you told your family about me?"

"A little," she said, "but I know they'll like you. especially my brother. He liked talking to you at the church."

A silence fell when we drove up in front of her house. It was an ordinary good farmhouse, nothing fancy, but it had everything needed to be comfortable. All her family was there to meet us. Her brother, sister, brother-in-law, mother, and daddy they were there to see what June brought home. We went in the living room and began to talk. I knew I was being checked out. Her mother and father were respectable with nice smiles.

June said, "I want to show Lloyd around a little before we eat."

Somebody agreed and reminded her they going to eat in about thirty minutes. June took me by the hand and lead me out of the room. We went outside to see several outbuildings. I saw an old outhouse that wasn't being used since a bathroom had been added to the house. There was a barn and we walked but didn't talk much . I did not know what to say.

Finally, I said, "I like your family. Do you like fried chicken?"

"Yeah, I sure do!"

She said, "Good. I bet that's what's for supper."

We headed back toward the house. She said, "Dad still runs the farm land and raises a few cows every year. He's sixty five years old and draws Social Security."

When we got back to the house I smelled fried chicken and my stomach growled.

Someone said, "We're ready to eat. If you want to wash up the bathroom is just down the hall."

The dining room table was a big nice table with a lot of food on it. I could see a big plate of biscuits. Her dad asked the blessing. We passed the food around and I took out a chicken leg, corn, and covered my biscuits with gravy. It was really good.

I said, "Fried chicken and hot biscuits with gravy can't be beat!" They agreed.

I knew they were still checking me out. After a while they began to ask me questions and I did too. By the end of the meal we were talking back and forth and I felt at ease. After eating, we went into the living room and June's sister took over washing the dishes. I asked June's dad what kind of cows he had. He was glad to talk about his Angus cows. I agree that they made good steaks with a grin. He shook his head yes.

When the talking died down June's sister said there was a bedroom upstairs for me and June could show me at any time I wanted to go. In a little while I told June that I was ready to turn in. The bedroom was, I guessed, the extra bedroom since her sister had married.

I gave June a kiss and asked, "Do you think I passed inspection?"

She smiled and said, "Yeah, I know they like you. I will see you in the morning."

It took me an hour or more before I went to sleep, but I slept good all night. When I woke up it was daylight and I could hear movement downstairs. I waited a while before going down. June and her mother had cooked a breakfast of eggs of country bacon and biscuits and a good cup of strong coffee. I bragged on the biscuits and June added that her mama always made good biscuits.

After breakfast I found out June and her sister were making plans for a big formal wedding. It didn't matter to me but if that's what she wanted it was all right with me. About eleven o'clock I head back to Albany to catch my plane back home. June was to stay the rest of the week. I think everything turned out fine.

Chapter 8

Back home I made plans for me and June to visit the Indian school on the weekend. That way she wouldn't have to miss school. On the following Saturday I met June in Nashville and we both got on a plane for Ashley, Wyoming. She was excited flying in the airplane for her first time. I rented a car and we drove around going to our motel. I had reserved two rooms. I knew that was the way she wanted it. After checking in, we sat around in my room until time to eat. We had spotted a restaurant where we wanted to eat. It was nice dim light soft music and a good meal.

We talked about a lot of stuff. I told her I wasn't interested in the hanging on to money. I just wanted to do something worthwhile . I didn't want to donate to an organization that had a lot of expense. Whatever I did I wanted it to be the two of us. I needed her. We went back to the motel and decided to turn in and get an early start in the morning. I lay on my bed and could not sleep, thinking how nice it would be for her to be in bed with me making love. The next morning I woke up to the radio playing country music. I got up, showered, and called her room at seven o'clock. She was ready, so we left and stopped at the fast-food restaurant for breakfast sandwiches and coffee.

When we got to the school, we met the Indian lady. I didn't know how to say her name. but she told him it was Clarissa FastHorse. She was anxious to show us around and show us their need, but she did not ask any questions. The children were all around playing simple games. June saw the out houses, the kitchen, and the water tank on the trailer . The children's clothes were worn and some needed new shoes. I told June the orphanage survived by donations of money my clothes and supplies . The Indian lady that ran the place didn't even get a salary beyond food and board. We know she is worth far more than that.

I found out that a group of volunteers, probably six, made up a board that decided what to do and we would need to get their permission before doing anything. When we left, June was quiet for a long time but I knew she was close to tears so I didn't ask anything.

When June finally spoke she had a lot to say. "Every living thing on this planet has to have water, both plants and animals. That place must have water to survive and thrive. Those children deserve better that what they have. There are a lot of places that need water just like them. With water they could have chickens and goats and even a small garden. They could help themselves. Giving them water is better than anything else. An everlasting well is the best thing anybody could give. It's something worth doing. Let's do it."

I said, "Thank you, June! Those are exactly my thoughts."

I called Mrs. Fasthorse and asked her to set up a meeting with the people that decide what to do and we headed back home .

June changed planes in Nashville and I hated to see her go. I gave her tight squeeze and a nice long kiss and I told her I loved her.

Chapter 8

The next day Mrs. FastHorse called and gave a date
and time the board would meet and asked if that was alright.
I told her we will be there. I called June and she said she
needed to stay in school and told me to go by myself. The
next day I headed back to Wyoming. This time I dressed up
a little more than I have in the past. I didn't want the board
to think I might start something and not finish it.

When I got to the meeting, I introduced myself and
explained about Jane. I let them know that Jane and I were
engaged to be married soon and we were in this together.
Some of the men had coats on . I suspected they dressed up
just for me. I told them we would like to pay for a digging a
well at the orphanage and, even though we were not sure we
could get water, we wanted to have their permission to try.

They all seemed happy and kept saying. "Yes, yes,
yes!"

I said. "Now if we do get water there will be a lot of changes at the school, and you can begin to think about that. But don't count on the water until you get it."

On the drive back to town I stopped by Mr. Webster's and told him what I was doing. He smiled and said, "That's a mighty good deed!"

I asked him to call his cousin and tell him to let me know when he could start. I left my phone on all the next day when I got home and waited for his call.

He said, "Man, you hit it lucky! I can start your well as soon as I finish the well I'm digging right now. I usually have people lined up."

I said, " That's good! Call me as soon as you are ready."

I called June that night and told her everything. She was pleased I could tell. Her graduation and our wedding were coming up soon. I was getting nervous. I didn't know what all they had planned but I knew that June would be a beautiful bride.

I told my sister about the well digging plan and about my wedding coming soon. She was glad I was involved in a good work they were helping support. She was excited about the wedding and eager to meet June. She and her husband planned on going to our wedding. My mother and dad have decided not to go for health reasons.

I go by the shop where I use to work on their dinner break. I knew the boss didn't like people coming in and interrupting their work, but they all seemed glad to see me. I missed working, I told them what I hoped to do for the orphanage and that I am soon to be a married man.

I began researching well digging machines. I found out who made them and how much do they cost. I study how they work and what the operator does. I found out the machines vary a lot depending on how deep it is digs and that different methods are used. I decided to talk it over with my well digger who had a lot of experience and I could learn a lot from him.

Chapter 9

The week before the wedding I had to get her a ring.
I had almost forgotten that part. June told me to wear a dark
blue suit if I had one for the wedding. I went to a nice
jewelry store and bought her a solid gold beautiful ring, not
too big and gaudy, but not too skimpy either. I believed it
would fit her character and we could select a diamond or
two later together. I decided that the nice suit I already had
would be fine. The graduation was to be on Saturday and the
wedding was planned for Sunday evening.

I catch an early flight to Albany on Saturday
morning. I rented a car and checked into a motel. The
graduation is at two o'clock. I killed time so I wouldn't get
to the school too early .

The ceremony was outside and I saw June's family
and walked over to them. They were glad to see me. I sat
beside June's brother who had a machine shop. He started
talking about his shop and I told him about my shop. He
said his shop was on the way home so we could stop and see

it. I agreed and followed him down the road. I thought he was given the task of entertaining me and bringing me to the wedding.

His shop was on the highway in a concrete black building with about forty feet by sixty feet, a nice little shop. He didn't have a lot of equipment and most of it was old, but I could see he was proud of it. I would be too.

When we got to his house I met his wife, Betty, who used a walker with wheels as a result of a car wreck injury. She was not going to the wedding. They gave me a nice comfortable bedroom. I lay on the bed thinking about the wedding and could not sleep. We had decided not to go on a honeymoon somewhere, but just go home to my house because we were anxious to hear from the well digger. That meant we would spend our first night in a motel room. I hope she won't feel bad about that.

We got to the church early. Mike had put our suitcases in my car and parked it in front of the church. I had my blue suit on with the carnation in the buttonhole. June was nowhere in sight but I knew she was somewhere in the church .

When it got almost time, I peeped out and church was full of people. Mike was my best man. June's dad gave her away. June was beautiful coming down that aisle smiling at everyone but especially at me. After we exchanged our vows the preacher pronounced us man and wife, I kissed my bride. I thought nothing could be better.

We put on regular clothes and when we got to the car, several people hugged June and shook my hand goodbye. Nothing was tied to the car and no rice was thrown because June knew that rice would kill birds if they ate it. I apologized for not going on a honeymoon. She smiled and told me it would be alright. When we got to the motel I was going to pick her up and carry her over the threshold but she shook her head and said that was for our home.

We went down the street and got a little to eat before going to bed. When we got back to the room I went in the bathroom and took a shower, cleaned up, and put on my pajamas. She looked at me and smiled. She went in the bathroom and stayed a long time period I got in bed. When she came out she was wearing a pretty loose fit gown. Beautiful.

She stood there by the bed as I looked at her. I reached out my hand and she took it and crawled in bed beside me. What a wonderful feeling to love someone and know they love you too.

That night was something I will remember the rest of my life.

The next morning we headed for the airport and home. My house was small but comfortable. She could see it needed a woman's touch.

Chapter 10

The next morning I called the older Mr. Webster to see if he had heard from his cousin. He told me the well digger had finished the job was on, but he had to do some repair on his equipment before going to the school. He didn't how that was going.

I took June to meet my mother and dad. They welcomed her into the family. Then I visited my sister. She and June had a good time just talking girl talk, like when they knew they were in love and how to change the house.

I called the Indian woman and she said the well diggers were moving their equipment onto the property. So we decided to go. We went by the store and bought some work clothes, Dress clothes would be out of the place around well digging.

The next morning we took our time traveling. The well digger does not need us. I would have gladly helped him if he had needed me. When we got to the school and drove in, we could hear the digging machine working. When Mr. Webster saw us, he stopped the machine and came over to greet us. I introduced June as my wife and partner. He liked June I could tell and I think he approved of our work clothes.

"I don't mind helping you if you need me," I said.

"He said, "Maybe," so I just watched.

Mrs. FastHorse came down by the well and I introduced June to her and they a little about the kids and she went back up the hill. A little later Mrs. FastHorse came down again and stretched a rope between two sticks. She and Mr. Webster had already had a conversation. The rope was about fifty feet from the well. As soon as the school was out all the children wanted to see what was going on and here they came. The Indian lady made sure they stayed behind the rope. Mr. Webster had easy digging and made good progress the first day because it was mostly clay.

We left early knowing everything was going fine. "Nothing we could do," I said. "Would you like to go by and see Mr. Webster, the old man who gave me advice?"

She said, "Yes. That will be fun."

When we pulled into his drive, sure enough, there he was sitting on the front porch with a big grin. June liked me visiting with him and talking. I knew he was lonesome with nobody to talked to all day. He liked June. I knew he would. Everybody liked June. I let him know we had just been married a few days and I told him what was going on at the school.

When we left, we drove around town a little before going to the motel. Mr.Webster, the well digger, said we should know before the week is out if it has water unless the digger hits hard rock. Then the diggers go slow.

June said. "Do you reckon we could find a furnished apartment with a kitchen so we could fix our own food?"

I said, "I don't know but that would be nice."

The next day we checked around and checked the paper and could not find an apartment like that. The next day we went back to the school. The digging is doing good but a little slower. The well casings needed be unloaded and lined up for installing. He had a gas-powered Ford truck with balloon tires. I told him I could drive the Ford truck and unload it for him and he agreed.

While I was unloading the truck. June went up and visited the school. The well digger kept digging. At the end of the day, Mr. Webster, looked at me. He knew I could work and didn't mind helping. I think I went up a little on that his evaluation of me. The next day I helped at the well and June was in the school. She was making friends with the children and the children were all around her.

Chapter 11

On the fourth day digging slowed down because they had hit hard rock . This continued through day five. I wondered if we had got a dry hole. I thought don't give up, keep going. On the sixth day drilling got easier. We got through the Hard Rock. In the afternoon Mr. Webster motioned for me to come down . He showed me some moisture. It was a good sign. A little later he hit water.

He said, "It looks good but don't count your chickens before they hatch. We've got to see what we have in volume. We have to put a pump in and to do that."

He had a gasoline pump to check it out. We went to my car and started blowing my horn. June and Mrs. FastHorse came outside and I motioned for them to come. The Indian lady went back in and dismissed school. So here came all the children. After he got the pump turned on nothing happened for a minute or two then one big squirt up in the air came, then nothing, then a continuous big squirt up in the air. Everybody was cheering. Mr. Webster went over with a fruit jar and collected a sample. He tasted it, looked at it, and found it crystal clear with no sulfur.

He walked over and handed it to us. I took a taste and handed it to June. She took a taste too. I look at her with a smile on my face and she smiled back. Mr. Webster said we could let the pump run a while to check the volume. In about twenty minutes he cut the pump off . We now had a small pond close to the well.

We needed to buy an electric pump. We are letting Mr. Webster tell us the best kind of buy size and what kind of voltage we need. We decided a high wattage pump will work best for the orphanage.

He said, "I can order it for you if you want. I can get a discount."

I said, "Yes that's good. Go ahead."

The next day we met with the board in charge of the school. I told them they needed to plan on what to do about the electricity needed by the pump.

I gave a little speech. "You need to call your electrician and have him install electricity at the pump as soon as possible and we will pay for it. You need to notify your donors and let them know about the well and ask for more help to put in all the plumbing needed. You need to make some long-term plans. You can get a mortgage that is not too much and doners will help. I will help. If you have an architect who is a donor, see if he would design you something for free."

The board nodded in agreement and then began saying how glad they were the children would have water and discussed who would take care of what task. I shook hands all around and left.

We went back to the motel at night, happy and pleased how things were working out. We said," Thank you, Lord, for giving us water."

Chapter 12

We went home the tenth day and waited for the pump to be installed. I started fixing up the house a little better while waiting to hear about the pump. I didn't know if they would get somebody that knows how to plan a school like that. I made a few drawings freehand like I thought they needed right now. I thought they would need a water tower with the reservoir tank, so they could have good fresh water pressure anywhere on site.

I wondered about the cost. So far we had spent less than what I expected. We could have spend some more, but I didn't want to put all my eggs in one basket. There were other projects out there that needed help.

Mr. Webster called and said the pump was being shipped. We needed to plan on a building a house for the pump. He suggested a twelve by twelve concrete pad around the well for a foundation for the well house I said that sounds good.

In about a week he called and said. "It's done and on a pad."

I said' "Good! We'll be there to check it out and settle up with you."

He said. "Ok. I'll see you at the school."

June and I were anxious to see what it looked like. I hoped he had the electricity attached to the pump and we could see it run. We got a plane the next day for Wyoming. We rented a car and headed for the school as soon as we could.

When we get to the school, we headed for the well first. The pump was setting in the middle of the concrete pad. There was a tarp over it and close by was an electric light pole with a temporary cable going into the pump. I uncovered the pump and saw an on and off switch. There was a one inch pipe coming from the pump with a cutoff valve . The pipe then went through the slab and into a ditch going away. At the end of the vertical pipe was a cut off valve.

I look at June, "You ready to try it out?"

She said, "Yeah, go ahead."

I opened both valves and turned it on. It began to run but no water came. I kept thinking. I bet it has to be primed but the sound of the changed. I said, "Now it's drawing water!"

. Sure enough, water began to squirt out of the faucet with good pressure. We cut off the pump, put the tarp back, and went up the hill to find the Indian lady. She was all smiles and said they were already using in the water from the spigot. I told her to set up a meeting with the people on the board as soon as they could. Mr. Webster had already removed all his equipment. The next day about two o'clock we met with the people in charge.

The architect wanted to know what they thought. He wanted to know how many children lived there and their ages in order match the design to the need. They had trouble deciding. I paid for the electrical work.

June spoke up and said, " There is work that needs to be done right now.to make the place better for the children."

It was decided to break up the work and do a temporary fix for a few years then work on a long-term plan. The children need bathrooms and a new kitchen now. June thought we could pay for that.

We went out to see Mr. Webster late that afternoon when he got home from work. He seemed glad to see us.

We thanked him for doing a good job. He handed us a piece of paper showing the result of the water analysis by a lab. The report was good. He then gave us his bill for digging the well, the pump, and for installing it with a concrete pad. He gave us some names of local contractors and plumbers we might employ. We wrote a check to Mr. Webster and paid him in full.

Now me and June had some work to do. On our way back to the motel we stopped at the store and get some papers and pencils . We needed to make a plan. We stopped at the fast food restaurant and picked up burgers and fries because we were anxious to start planning what to do.

I made a rough layout of the well and locations of the dormitories and kitchen. By nine o'clock we had a plan on what to do. Since the pump and the reservoir that would need to maintain pressure for a little while when the pump wasn't working. We did not need a big tank on the tower. The building was on a plain Gable roof building . So we just had to just add on to the end of each building. We had a one and a half inch diameter pipe to each building, then a three quarter inch pipe into each building. The sewer line would go to the common septic tank and drain well make a concrete block to house around the well

We wondered if we should we take the plans to the people in charge and got their approval. If we do that it might slow us down since five or six people cannot decide just like that. We decide to go on ahead and get it done. After all we were paying for it. We made a drawing good enough to show the contractors but not to scale and a lot of notes on type of construction required.

. The next day we got copies made and contracted the people Mr. Webster recommended. With that done we had nothing to do we decided to go out to see the old Mr. Webster. He was glad to see us as always. He liked June as well as me, I thought. We tell him about what we are doing he seemed very interested. I told him if he wanted to see the place we would be glad to take him. and he said he might later on but not that day.

A couple of days later we picked up several quotes from contractors. We were impressed with one of the quotes. It was for everything they had drawn to scale with dimensions. It was typed and listed everything. All the others were just for parts of it and not clear what they intended to do. We decided to go with the one that did it all . It was a little more pricey, but we believed it to be the best deal.

Chapter 13

We went home the next day. June wanted to go to her parents' home and visit. I was glad to do that. On our way to Albany we are very happy, talking about what we're doing. June said she misses seeing the children.

They treated me well too. We put on some comfortable old clothes and went for a walk and noticed chickens running around the barn. We wonder if the school would try to have chickens or any other animals. We decided they have got to do for themselves. We take a long walk around the farm and out through some woods. The house was a good comfortable place. When we got back June went into the kitchen with her mother. I stretched out on the bed and it felt so good I kept lying there. Before I knew it, I was asleep. When I woke up and looked at the clock I knew I had slept. June and her mother fixed supper for us and June's sister and her husband who came to see us.

Judging by the smell in the house I knew the good supper was coming.

We told them all we had been doing. June did most of the talking. It showed that she very much enjoyed what we are doing. I was glad to hear that as I had been afraid she was just doing it for my sake. The supper was really good. June had told her mother I liked milk gravy and there was a table with a big bowl of gravy and lots of biscuits. I could see your mother was pleased when I asked someone to pass the gravy the second time.

I had some good conversation with June's dad. He asked a lot of questions and told me a lot of things he had done in his life. We both felt at ease talking with each other. June's sister and husband went home at eight thirty and we all went to bed about nine o'clock.

We went to sleep with their arms around each other. What a good feeling to love someone that also loves you. The next morning I left June to visit with her mother and I drove over to her brother's shop. He was glad to see me and showed me around his shop. I saw a lot of real good work he was doing.

I asked him, "Are there was some manufacturing plants around here?"

He said. " No, but there are several in Albany."

I said, "Well, that's not too far away. You can get lots more for your job in a manufacturing plant."

"I know," he said.

I took my time driving back to the house since it was a good pleasant drive. I like the countryside. When I got to the house, June's dad was sitting on the front porch so I sat down close to him. We talked a little about where I had been and what I had seen. Mostly we just sat there not talking, but it was peaceful. We were watching a squirrel run up and down a tree in the yard. The next day we headed for home, our talk turned to work on the orphanage.

June said, "When they start the footings you can go by yourself. I need to do some work on the house."

I said, "I'll miss you, but do whatever you want with the house."

I started looking at the paper for a used camper or motorhome thinking that would allow me to stay at the school. I don't like any I see. Then I realize I don't need to buy a used one. I can afford a new one.

June and I talked it over . If we buy a nice motorhome, we both could stay at the school, cook her own food, and when the job is over, we can take some trips, also, we might be able to get some tax relief. After looking at several we decide on a motorhome. I found a nice one, but it cost more money than I wanted to spend. I had to have it.

We both laughed when June teased me, "You are still a boy wanting a new toy."

Chapter 14

When they started the footing on the new buildings, I left to go there in the motorhome. It was easy to drive and ran good. I learned to make wide turns. I stopped several times in big parking lots, fixed a little to eat, and lay down to rest in the motorhome. I loved it.

When I got to the school they were pouring the footings for the two restrooms in the kitchen. An open ditch was ready for the water lines. It was going just right. They knew what they were doing and not wasting any time. I checked in with Mrs. FastHorse. She had noticed the motorhome. I told her I would be staying in there that night. The kids came around to look at a house that someone could drive, but I didn't invite them inside, but I told them about it. I thought June might want to bring a few kids at a time inside when she came.

The next day no workers came but concrete blocks were delivered, plus sand and mortar. The next morning early I heard noise outside. It was the masonry crew. They went right to work. They built an eight foot block wall around the edge of the well pad. Space for two windows and a space for a metal door frame were left open. Then they built foundation walls for the bathroom in the kitchen. It went fast. The easy block laying was all done by the end of the day.

I called June on my cell phone and told her everything. The next two days nothing was done except lumber and material were delivered. I was bored so I visited the school and began to get to know some of the older boys. I did not want to show any of them, the children or Mrs. FastHorse the motorhome. I did not want to appear bragging about what I have. The next day the contractor was there with several carpenters. We talked. I told him that it looked good and he just nodded his head yes. He didn't waste any time with me. He went on about his business. I like that. The school let out early and they all came out to watch with me. Mrs. FastHorse had put out some boundary markers and the children had to stay behind the markers.

The children were learning how things were made. It was my hope that the older boys would build some things around the school after we leave, like maybe a chicken house or pen. I was bored and I didn't know why I was staying here. They didn't need me and I missed June so I decided to head for home.

I got home and went inside. What a surprise! Is this my house with new carpet, window curtains and a new table? June stood there and smiled. It looked like a woman lived there. I hugged and kissed her and told her I missed her so much I had to go home early. She was glad to see me too.

We waited a week before going back to the school. We stopped about halfway there at a rest area. June cooked sausage and eggs and I made coffee. We enjoyed a good snack then I went and lay down on the bed to rest in a few minutes. June came and lay down beside me and we hugged each other. We were happy when we wake up two hours later. June wanted to drive. She did fine, but she needed to learn how to turn sharp curves. It's better if two can drive.

Chapter 15

When we got to the school all the buildings were up with roofs but no shingles. The pipe in the ground were covered up. Going by the number of cars around the buildings I knew they were working on the inside. We went to the well house first. A nice metal door and two insulated windows had been installed. One inch thick foam insulation boards were attached to the inside walls. The metal roof had fiberglass insulation.

We went to the boys' dormitory. The men are still working, but we can see two urinals and three commodes. Drywall was done but not painted. They have a long common shower. We were told they were going to make the commode partitions with plywood doors.. The floors would had vinyl covering.

There was not as much done on the girls' dormitory. Looking at the plans, I saw it was going to be a little better than the boys' dormitory with a tile floor and nice sinks with mirrors.

When we looked in the kitchen and saw men working on it. A lot of thought had gone into in the kitchen. Tile covered the floor and up the wall for five feet. Drains were in the floors. A nice grill with a galvanized hood over it was on one wall. Two refrigerators and a big stove with an oven were on another wall. A large worktable with a stainless steel top stood in the middle. A dishwasher had been ordered but had not arrived yet.

As we walked back to our motorhome June thought out loud, "There are going to be a lot of changes at the school. That's good. It sure was something worth doing!"

"Something worthwhile!!" beamed Lloyd.

About the Author

These stories were written my Aunt Lucy's husband, Uncle Lucius Agree. Both grew up in different parts of rural hill county northeast of Nashville. With values intact, both moved to Nashville, met one another and fell into an enduring love. Their work ethic led them into successful business ventures while raising three sons and a daughter.

In their later years, at age ninety plus, they moved to an assisted living home with restricted freedom. Aunt Lucy (Alene Massey Agee) read many books to fill her time. After his WW11 biography, *I Remember*, was published, Uncle Lucius took up his pencil and began to write. He was convinced that the stories he authored were as interesting as some of the short stories Aunt Lucy read.

Uncle Lucius has exposed his heart and soul in these stories which, no doubt, reflect his real life experiences disguised in the thoughts and actions of his fictional characters.

Maxie Massey Fortner, Typist with minimal editing and Publisher

—

Made in the USA
Monee, IL
16 July 2021

73728681R00075